É

The illustrations in this book were rendered in pen and ink and watercolor.

Book design by Carrie Leeb.
Typeset in Bernhard Modern and Garamond 3.
Printed in Hong Kong.

Library of Congress Cataloging-in-Publication Data

London, Jonathan, 1947–
Condor's egg/by Jonathan London; illustrated by James Chaffee; afterword by Robert Mesta.
p.   cm.
Summary: The last two California Condors living in the wild hatch an egg.
ISBN 0-8118-0260-4
1. California condor—Juvenile fiction. [1. California condor—Fiction. 2. Condors—Fiction.
3. Rare birds—Fiction. 4 Endangered species—Fiction.] I. Chaffee, James, ill. II. Title.
PZ10.3.L8534Co   1994
[E]—dc20   93-31001
                                                  AC

Distributed in Canada by Raincoast Books
112 East Third Avenue, Vancouver, B.C. V5T 1C8

10 9 8 7 6 5 4 3 2 1

Chronicle Books
275 Fifth Street
San Francisco, California 94103

Condor's Egg

written by Jonathan London   illustrated by James Chaffee
afterword by Robert Mesta

Chronicle Books * San Francisco

Among the rugged slopes of inland cliffs,
there live two California Condors.

One condor flies, soaring high in the sky.
Circling, he rides the warm air,
higher than the tops of the clouds.

Companion of the sun and wind,
friend of the wild mountain silence,
he sails above the high, lonely cliffs.

He glides over a hidden lake nestled
like an egg, far, far below. The condor
tilts and circles, sliding down the wind
out of the blinding sun.

Carrion-eater.
Bone-picker.
Nature's cleaner-upper,
feathered giant of the sky.

After his meal, the great bird of prey
plows through the air to his high cliff cave.

There his mate arranges a ring of pebbles
around the egg: a jewel, so fragile, flawless.

They wait, taking turns keeping their egg warm.

In the night a storm brews.
Black clouds boil up.
Thunder rumbles and growls
and electric branches
illuminate the sky.

Suddenly a bolt of jagged fire
strikes above the condors' cave
with a terrible crash.
Rocks tumble and crumble.
With an explosion of wings and
feathers, the condors flail and flap.

When the dust and feathers clear, the egg is cracked
with a fine zig-zag line like a jab of lightning.

The two condors settle together above the egg.
Is this the end—or the beginning—of a new life?

All night the wind roars and lashes rain at the cave's door.
And throughout the storm, the lightning cracks open
the night sky like an enormous black egg.

But by dawn, the storm is over; the sky is clear.
The sun enters and warms the cave.

And by morning, something begins to stir within the condor's egg.
First a beak. Then a talon. Then a wet, bald head pushes through.

Finally, the whole wobbly chick, looking dazed by the light.

As mother and father condor gently nuzzle her, the baby stretches her scrawny wings for the very first time.

In less than a year, she will be able to fly. She will sail among the clouds, companion of the sun and wind.

Another feathered giant of the sky.

More About Condors

The California Condor is the rarest and largest bird in North America, and one of the largest in the world. It can weigh twenty-two pounds and have a wingspan of nine feet. When seen from a distance, it is often mistaken for a small plane.

Condors spend most of their daylight hours soaring on winds in search of food. They can glide as far as ten miles without moving their wings, and single day flights of up to one hundred miles have been reported. They nest in shallow caves on the faces of steep cliffs. Pairs mate for life, and lay one egg every other year. In the wild, condors have lived to be fifty years of age.

Over ten thousand years ago, condors soared over the prehistoric wilderness, feeding on the carcasses of woolly mammoths, giant ground sloths and saber-toothed tigers. Unlike its prey, condors survived to be revered by the early human inhabitants of this land. The importance of the condor to native peoples was recorded in oral legends and rock paintings. The medicine men of the early Chumash Indians of Southern California wore ceremonial capes made of condor feathers, which were believed to give the power to travel to the "other world." While there, they hoped to obtain a spirit helper, which sometimes came to them in the form of a condor. It was believed that this spirit helper would give the medicine men wisdom to help their people.

The coming of modern civilization brought many changes to the condor's range. Originally the condor could be found all across North America, but by the seventeenth century its range was confined to the Southwest. And by the start of this century, it was found only in Southern California. Because of the loss of its habitat, illegal shooting and poisoning, the condor was soon at the brink of extinction. 1986 was the last year a pair of condors hatched an egg in the wild, and on Easter Sunday, 1987, in an attempt to save the species, the last free-flying condor was brought in from the wild. For the first time in thousands of years, the condor no longer graced the skies of North America. Only twenty-seven remained, all living in zoos.

Only five years later, due to the success of the captive breeding program, the population of California Condors had nearly doubled, and two young chicks were released into the wild. One was named *Xewe*, which means "to cast a shadow," and the other *Chocuyens*, which means "valley of the moon." Coincidentally, Xewe is the offspring of the last male condor to be brought in from the wild, and Chocuyens is the offspring of the last female to be brought in from the wild. It seems only fitting that the last pair of free-flying condors should be the parents of the first condors to return to the wild. It is hoped that one day these feathered giants will once again be seen flying freely across the skies of North America.

–Robert Mesta, Condor Recovery Program Coordinator

For more California Condor information, write to:

California Condor Recovery Program
U.S. Fish and Wildlife Service
2493-A Portola Road
Ventura, CA 93003

California Department of Fish and Game
1416 Ninth Street, Room 1280
Sacramento, CA 95814

U.S. Forest Service
Los Padres National Forest
6144 Calle Real
Goleta, CA 93117

San Diego Zoo
P.O. Box 551
San Diego, CA 92112

Los Angeles Zoo
5333 Zoo Drive
Los Angeles, CA 90017

The Peregrine Fund
World Center for Birds of Prey
566 W. Flying Hawk Lane
Boise, ID 83709

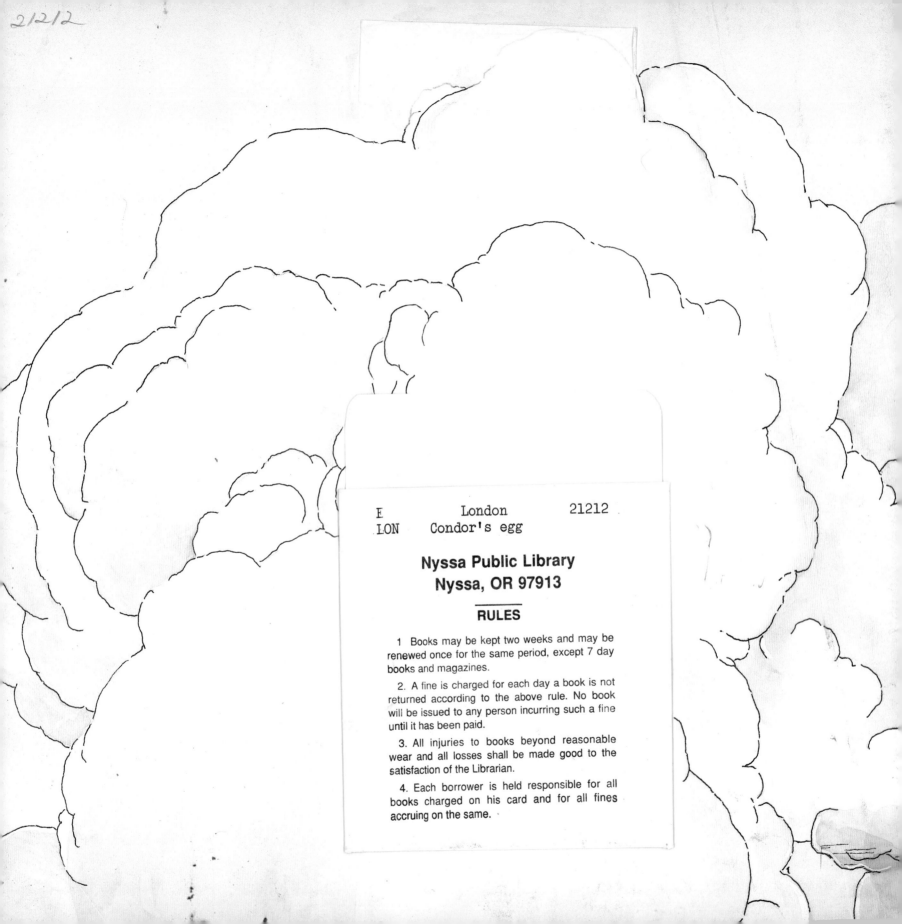